The Indian Emperor

John Dryden

Connection of The Indian Emperor to The Indian Queen
Prologue
Dramatis Personæ
Act I *Scene I—A pleasant Indian country Scene II—A Temple*
Act II *Scene I—The Magicians Cave Scene II Scene III—Changes to the Indian country Scene IV*
Act III *Scene I—A Chamber Royal Scene II—A camp Scene III Scene IV—Mexico*
Act IV *Scene I—A prison Scene II—Chamber-royal Scene III Scene IV—A prison*
Act V *Scene I—A chamber royal, an Indian hammock discovered in it Scene II—A prison*
Epilogue

John Dryden (19 August [O.S. 9 August] 1631 – 12 May [O.S. 1 May] 1700) was an English poet, literary critic, translator, and playwright who was made England's first Poet Laureate in 1668.

He is seen as dominating the literary life of Restoration England to such a point that the period came to be known in literary circles as the Age of Dryden. Walter Scott called him "Glorious John".

Early life:

Dryden was born in the village rectory of Aldwincle near Thrapston in Northamptonshire, where his maternal grandfather was rector of All Saints. He was the eldest of fourteen children born to Erasmus Dryden and wife Mary Pickering, paternal grandson of Sir Erasmus Dryden, 1st Baronet (1553–1632), and wife Frances Wilkes, Puritan landowning gentry who supported the Puritan cause and Parliament. He was a second cousin once removed of Jonathan Swift. As a boy Dryden lived in the nearby village of Titchmarsh, where it is likely that he received his first education. In 1644 he was sent to Westminster School as a King's Scholar where his headmaster was Dr. Richard Busby, a charismatic teacher and severe disciplinarian.[3] Having recently been re-founded by Elizabeth I, Westminster during this period embraced a very different religious and political spirit encouraging royalism and high Anglicanism. Whatever Dryden's response to this was, he clearly respected the headmaster and would later send two of his sons to school at Westminster.

As a humanist public school, Westminster maintained a curriculum which trained pupils in the art of rhetoric and the presentation of arguments for both sides of a given issue. This is a skill which would remain with Dryden and influence his later writing and thinking, as much of it displays these dialectical patterns. The Westminster curriculum included weekly translation assignments which developed Dryden's capacity for assimilation. This was also to be exhibited in his later works. His years at Westminster were not uneventful, and his first published poem, an elegy with a strong royalist feel on the death of his schoolmate Henry, Lord Hastings from smallpox, alludes to the execution of King Charles I, which took place on 30 January 1649, very near the school where Dr. Busby had first prayed for the King and then locked in his schoolboys to prevent their attending the spectacle.

In 1650 Dryden went up to Trinity College, Cambridge. Here he would have experienced a return to the religious and political ethos of his childhood: the Master of Trinity was a Puritan preacher by the name of Thomas Hill who had been a rector in Dryden's home village.[5] Though there is little specific information on Dryden's undergraduate years, he would most certainly have followed the standard curriculum of classics, rhetoric, and mathematics. In 1654 he obtained his BA, graduating top of the list for Trinity that year. In June of the same year Dryden's father died, leaving him some land which generated a little income, but not enough to live on.Returning to London during the Protectorate, Dryden obtained work with Cromwell's Secretary of State, John Thurloe. This appointment may have been the result of influence exercised on his behalf by his cousin the Lord Chamberlain, Sir Gilbert Pickering. At Cromwell's funeral on 23 November 1658 Dryden processed with the Puritan poets John Milton and Andrew Marvell. Shortly thereafter he published his first important poem, Heroic Stanzas (1658), a eulogy on Cromwell's death which is cautious and prudent in its emotional display. In 1660 Dryden celebrated the Restoration of the monarchy and the return of Charles II with Astraea Redux, an authentic royalist panegyric. In this work the interregnum is illustrated as a time of anarchy, and Charles is seen as the restorer of peace and order.

CONNECTION
OF
THE INDIAN EMPEROR
TO
THE INDIAN QUEEN

The conclusion of the Indian Queen (part of which poem was writ by me) left little matter for another story to be built on, there remaining but two of the considerable characters alive, viz. Montezuma and Orazia. Thereupon the author of this thought it necessary to produce new persons from the old ones: and considering the late Indian Queen, before she loved Montezuma, lived in clandestine marriage with her general Traxalla, from those two he has raised a son and two daughters, supposed to be left young orphans at their death. On the other side, he has has given to Montezuma and Orazia, two sons and a daughter; all now supposed to be grown up to men's and women's estate; and their mother, Orazia (for whom there was no further use in the story), lately dead.

So that you are to imagine about twenty years elapsed since the coronation of Montezuma; who, in the truth of the history, was a great and glorious prince; and in whose time happened the discovery and invasion of Mexico, by the Spaniards, under the conduct of Hernando Cortez, who joining with the Traxallan Indians, the inveterate enemies of Montezuma, wholly subverted that flourishing empire;—the conquest of which is the subject of this dramatic poem.

I have neither wholly followed the story, nor varied from it; and, as near as I could, have traced the native simplicity and ignorance of the Indians, in relation to European customs;—the shipping, armour, horses, swords, and guns of the Spaniards, being as new to them, as their habits and their language were to the Christians.

The difference of their religion from ours, I have taken from the story itself; and that which you find of it in the first and fifth acts, touching the sufferings and constancy of Montezuma in his opinions, I have only illustrated, not altered, from those who have written of it.

PROLOGUE.

Almighty critics! whom our Indians here
Worship, just as they do the devil—for fear,
In reverence to your power, I come this day,
To give you timely warning of our play.
The scenes are old, the habits are the same
We wore last year, before the Spaniards came.
Now, if you stay, the blood, that shall be shed
From this poor play, be all upon your head.
We neither promise you one dance, or show;
Then plot, and language, they are wanting too:
But you, kind wits, will those light faults excuse,
Those are the common frailties of the muse;
Which, who observes, he bays his place too dear;
For 'tis your business to be cozened here.
These wretched spies of wit must then confess,
They take more pains to please themselves the less.
Grant us such judges, Phoebus, we request,
As still mistake themselves into a jest;
Such easy judges, that our poet may
Himself admire the fortune of his play;
And, arrogantly, as his fellows do,
Think he writes well, because he pleases you,
This he conceives not hard to bring about,
If all of you would join to help him out:
Would each man take but what he understands,
And leave the rest upon the poet's hands.

DRAMATIS PERSONÆ.
INDIAN MEN.

Montezuma, *Emperor of Mexico.* Odmar, *his eldest son.* Guyomar, *his younger son.*
Orbellan, *son to the late Indian Queen by* Traxalla. *High Priest of the Sun.*
WOMEN.

Cydaria, *Montezuma's daughter.*
Almeria, SPECIAL_IMAGE-
OPS/images/c21_948ffc0712d721fae25ba425e142ce716d66f365.svg-REPLACE_ME *Sisters;
and daughters to the late Indian Queen.* Alibech,   SPANIARDS.

Cortez, *the Spanish General.*
Vasquez, SPECIAL_IMAGE-
OPS/images/c21_948ffc0712d721fae25ba425e142ce716d66f365.svg-REPLACE_ME
Commanders under him. Pizarro,   SCENE—*Mexico, and two leagues about it.*

THE
INDIAN EMPEROR.

ACT I.

SCENE I.—A pleasant Indian country.

Enter Cortez, Vasquez, Pizarro, *with Spaniards and Indians in their party.*

Cort. On what new happy climate are we thrown, So long kept secret, and so lately known; As if our old world modestly withdrew, And here in private had brought forth a new?

Vasq. Corn, wine, and oil, are wanting to this ground, In which our countries fruitfully abound; As if this infant world, yet unarrayed, Naked and bare in Nature's lap were laid. No useful arts have yet found footing here, But all untaught and savage does appear.

Cort. Wild and untaught are terms which we alone Invent, for fashions differing from our own ; For all their customs are by nature wrought, But we, by art, unteach what nature taught

Piz. In Spain, our springs, like old men's children, be Decayed and withered from the infancy: No kindly showers fall on our barren earth, To hatch the season in a timely birth : Our summer such a russet livery wears, As in a garment often dyed appears.

Cort. Here nature spreads her fruitful sweetness round, Breathes on the air, and broods upon the ground: Here days and nights the only seasons be; The sun no climate does so gladly see: When forced from hence, to view our parts, he mourns, Takes little journeys, and makes quick returns.

Vasq. Methinks, we walk in dreams on Fairyland, Where golden ore lies mixt with common sand; Each downfall of a flood, the mountains pour From their rich bowels, rolls a silver shower.

Cort. Heaven from all ages wisely did provide This wealth, and for the bravest nation hide, Who, with four hundred foot and forty horse, Dare boldly go a new-found world to force.

Piz. Our men, though valiant, we should find too few, But Indians join the Indians to subdue; Traxallan, shook by Montezuma's powers, Has, to resist his forces, called in ours.

Vasq. Rashly to arm against so great a king, I hold not safe; nor is it just to bring A war without a fair defiance made.

Piz. Declare we first our quarrel; then invade.

Cort. Myself, my king's ambassador will go; Speak, Indian guide, how far to Mexico ?

Ind. Your eyes can scarce so far a prospect make, As to discern the city on the lake; But that broad causeway will direct your way, And you may reach the town by noon of day.

Cort. Command a party of our Indians out, With a strict charge, not to engage, but scout: By noble ways we conquest will prepare; First, offer peace, and, that refused, make war.

[*Exeunt*

SCENE II.—*A Temple.*

The High Priest with other Priests. To them an Indian.

Ind. Haste, holy priest, it is the king's command.
High Pr. When sets he forward?
Ind. He is near at hand.
High Pr. The incense is upon the altar placed, The bloody sacrifice already past; Five hundred captives saw the rising sun, Who lost their light ere half his race was run. That which remains we here must celebrate; Where, far from noise, without the city gate, The peaceful power that governs love repairs, To feast upon soft vows and silent prayers. We for his royal presence only stay, To end the rites of this so solemn day.

[*Exit Ind.*

Enter Montezuma; *his eldest son*, Odmar; *his daughter*, Cydaria; Almeria, Alibech, Orbellan, *and Train. They place themselves.* *High Pr.* On your birthday, while we sing To our gods and to our king, Her, among this beauteous quire, Whose perfections you admire, Her who fairest does appear, Crown her queen of all the year, Of the year and of the day, And at her feet your garland lay.
Odm. My father this way does his looks direct Heaven grant, he give it not where I suspect!

[Montezuma *rises, goes about the Ladies, and at length stays at* Almeria, *and bows.*

Mont. Since my Orazia's death, I have not seen A beauty so deserving to be queen As fair Almeria.
Alm. Sure he will not know

[*To her brother and sister, aside.*

My birth I to that injured princess owe, Whom his hard heart not only love denied, But in her sufferings took unmanly pride.
Alib. Since Montezuma will his choice renew, In dead Orazia's room electing you, 'Twill please our mother's ghost that you succeed To all the glories of her rival's bed.
Alm. If news be carried to the shades below, The Indian queen will be more pleased, to know, That I his scorns on him, who scorned her, pay.
Orb. Would you could right her some more noble way!

[*She turns to him, who is kneeling all this while.*

Mont. Madam, this posture is for heaven designed,

[*Kneeling.*

And what moves heaven I hope may make you kind.
Alm. Heaven may be kind, the gods uninjured live, And crimes below cost little to forgive: By thee, inhuman, both my parents died; One by thy sword, the other by thy pride.

Mont. My haughty mind no fate could ever bow, Yet must I stoop to one, who scorns me now: Is there no pity to my sufferings due?

Alm. As much as what my mother found from you.

Mont. Your mother's wrongs a recompence shall meet; I lay my sceptre at her daughter's feet

Alm. He, who does now my least commands obey, Would call me queen, and take my power away.

Odm. Can he hear this, and not his fetters break? Is love so powerful, or his soul so weak? I'll fright her from it—Madam, though you see The king is kind, I hope your modesty Will know, what distance to the crown is due.

Alm. Distance and modesty prescribed by you!

Odm. Almeria dares not think such thoughts as these.

Alm. She dares both think and act what thoughts she please. 'Tis much below me on his throne to sit; But when I do, you shall petition it

Odm. If, sir, Almeria does your bed partake, I mourn for my forgotten mother's sake.

Mont. When parents'loves are ordered by a son, Let streams prescribe theirfountains where to run.

Odm. In all I urge, I keep my duty still, Not rule your reason, but instruct your will.

Mont. Small use of reason in that prince is shown, Who follows others, and neglects his own.

[Almeria *to* Orbellan *and* Alibech, *who are this while whispering to her.*

Alm. No, he shall ever love, and always be The subject of my scorn and cruelty.

Orb. To prove the lasting torment of his life, You must not be his mistress, but his wife. Few know what care an husband's peace destroys, His real griefs, and his dissembled joys.

Alm. What mark of pleasing vengeance could be shown, If I, to break his quiet, lose my own?

Orb. A brother's life upon your love relies, Since I do homage to Cydaria's eyes: How can her father to my hopes be kind, If in your heart he no example find?

Alm. To save your life I'll suffer any thing, Yet I'll not flatter this tempestuous king; But work his stubborn soul a nobler way, And, if he love, I'll force him to obey. I take this garland, not as given by you,

[*To* Mont.

But as my merit and my beauty's due. As for the crown, that you, my slave, possess, To share it with you would but make me less.

Enter Guyomar *hastily.*

Odm. My brother Guyomar! methinks I spy Haste in his steps, and wonder in his eye.

Mont. I sent thee to the frontiers; quickly tell The cause of thy return ; are all things well?

Guy. I went, in order, sir, to your command, To view the utmost limits of the land: To that sea-shore where no more world is found, But foaming billows breaking on the ground; Where, for a while, my eyes no object met, But distant skies, that in the ocean set; And low-hung clouds, that dipt themselves in rain, To shake their fleeces on the earth again. At last, as far as I could cast my eyes Upon the sea, somewhat, methought, did rise, Like bluish mists, which, still appearing more, Took dreadful shapes, and moved towards the shore.

Mont. What forms did these new wonders represent?

Guy. More strange than what your wonder can invent The object, I could first distinctly view, Was tall straight trees, which on the waters flew; Wings on their sides, instead of leaves, did grow, AVhich gathered all the breath the winds could blow: And at their roots grew floating palaces, Whose outblowed bellies cut the yielding seas.

Mont. What divine monsters, O ye gods, were these, That float in air, and fly upon the seas! Came they alive, or dead, upon the shore?

Guy. Alas, they lived too sure: I heard them roar. All turned their sides, and to each other spoke ; I saw their words break out in fire and smoke. Sure 'tis their voice, that thunders from on high, Or these the younger brothers of the sky. Deaf with the noise, I took my hasty flight; No mortal courage can support the fright

High Pr. Old prophecies foretell our fall at hand, When bearded men in floating castles land. I fear it is of dire portent.

Mont. Go see What it foreshows, and what the gods decree. Meantime proceed we to what rites remain.— Odmar, of all this presence does contain, Give her your wreath, whom you esteem most fair.

Odm. Above the rest I judge one beauty rare. And may that beauty prove as kind to me,

                                        [*He gives* Ambech the wreath.

As I am sure fair Alibech is she.

Mont. You, Guyomar, must next perform your part.

Guy. I want a garland, but I 'll give a heart: My brother's pardon I must first implore, Since I with him fair Alibech adore.

Odm. That all should Alibech adore, 'tis true; But some respect is to my birthright due. My claim to her by eldership I prove.

Guy. Age is a plea in empire, not in love.

Odm. I long have stayed for this solemnity, To make my passion public.

Guy. So have I.

Odm. But from her birth my soul has been her slave; My heart received the first wounds which she gave: I watched the early glories of her eyes, As men for daybreak watch the eastern skies.

Guy. It seems my soul then moved the quicker pace; Yours first set out, mine reached her in the race.

Mont. Odmar, your choice I cannot disapprove; Nor justly, Guyomar, can blame your love. To Alibech alone refer your suit, And let her sentence finish your dispute.

Alib. You think me, sir, a mistress quickly won, So soon to finish what is scarce begun: In this surprise should I a judgment make, 'Tis answering riddles ere I 'm well awake: If you oblige me suddenly to choose, The choice is made, for I must both refuse: For to myself I owe this due regard, Not to make love my gift, but my reward. Time best will show, whose services will last

Odm. Then judge my future service by my past What I shall be, by what I was, you know: That love took deepest root, which first did grow.

Guy. That love, which first was set, will first decay; Mine, of a fresher date, will longer stay.

Odm. Still you forget my birth.

Guy. But you, I see, Take care still to refresh my memory.

Mont. My sons, let your unseemly discord cease, If not in friendship, live at least in peace. Orbellan, where you love, bestow your wreath.

Orb. My love I dare not, even in whispers, breathe.

Mont. A virtuous love may venture any thing.

Orb. Not to attempt the daughter of my king.

Mont. Whither is all my former fury gone? Once more I have Traxalla's chains put on, And by his children am in triumph led: Too well the living have revenged the dead!

Alm. You think my brother born your enemy; He's of Traxalla's blood, and so am I.

Mont. In vain I strive. My lion-heart is with love's toils beset; Struggling I fall still deeper in the net Cydaria, your new lover's garland take, And use him kindly for your father's sake.

Cyd. So strong an hatred does my nature sway, That, spite of duty, I must disobey; Besides, you warned me still of loving two; Can I love him, already loving you?

Enter a Guard hastily.

Mont. You look amazed, as if some sudden fear Had seized your hearts; is any danger near?

1 *Guard.* Behind the covert, where this temple stands Thick as the shades, there issue swarming bands Of ambushed men, whom, by their arms and dress, To be Traxallan enemies I guess.

2 *Guard.* The temple, sir, is almost compassed round.

Mont. Some speedy way for passage must be found. Make to the city by the postern gate, I'll either force my victory, or fate; A glorious death in arms I 'll rather prove, Than stay to perish tamely by my love.

[*Exeunt.*

An alarm within. Enter Montezuma, Odmar, Guyomar, Alibech, Orbellan, Cydaria, Almeria, *as pursued by Traxallans.*   *Mont.* No succour from the town?

Odm. None, none is nigh.

Guy. We are enclosed, and must resolve to die.

Mont. Fight for revenge, now hope of life is past; But one stroke more, and that will be my last.

Enter Cortez, Vasquez, Pizarro, *to the Traxallans:* Cortez *stays them just falling on.*   *Cort.* Contemned? my orders broke even in my sight? Did I not strictly charge, you should not fight?

[*To his Indians.*

Ind. Your choler, general, does unjustly rise, To see your friends pursue your enemies. The greatest and most cruel foes we have, Are these, whom you would ignorantly save. By ambushed men, behind their temple laid, We have the king of Mexico betrayed.

Cort. Where, banished virtue, wilt thou shew thy face, If treachery infects thy Indian race? Dismiss your rage, and lay your weapons by: Know I protect them, and they shall not die.

Ind. O wondrous mercy, shown to foes distrest!

Cort. Call them not so, when once with odds opprest; Nor are they foes my clemency defends, Until they have refused the name of friends : Draw up our Spaniards by themselves, then fire Our guns on all, who do not straight retire.

[*To Vasq.*

Ind. O mercy, mercy! at thy feet we fall,

[*Indians kneeling.*

Before thy roaring Gods destroy us all: See, we retreat without the least reply; Keep thy Gods silent! if they speak, we die.

[*The Traxallans retire.*

Mont. The fierce Traxallans lay their weapons down, Some miracle in our relief is shown.

Guy. These bearded men in shape and colour be Like those I saw come floating on the sea.

[Mont, *kneels to* Cort.

Mont. Patron of Mexico and God of wars, Son of the sun, and brother of the stars——

Cort. Great monarch, your devotion you misplace.

Mont. Thy actions show thee born of heavenly race. If then thou art that cruel God, whose eyes Delight in blood, and human sacrifice, Thy dreadful altars.I with slaves will store, And feed thy nostrils with hot reeking gore; Or if that mild and gentle God thou be, Who dost mankind below with pity see, With breath of incense I will glad thy heart; But if, like us, of mortal seed thou art, Presents of choicest fowls and fruits I'll bring, And in my realms thou shalt be more than king.

Cort. Monarch of empires, and deserving more Than the sun sees upon your western shore; Like you a man, and hither led by fame, Not by constraint, but by my choice, I came; Ambassador of peace, if peace you choose, Or herald of a war if you refuse.

Mont. Whence, or from whom, dost thou these offers bring?

Cort. From Charles the Fifth, the world's most potent king.

Mont. Some petty prince and one of little fame, For to this hour I never heard his name: The two great empires of the world I know, That of Peru, and this of Mexico; And since the earth none larger does afford, This Charles is some poor tributary lord.

Cort. You speak of that small part of earth you know; But betwixt us and you wide oceans flow, And wat'ry deserts of so vast extent, That passing hither four full moons we spent

Mont. But say, what news, what offers dost thou bring From so remote, and so unknown a king ?

[*While* Vasquez *speaks,* Cortez *spies the ladies and goes to them, entertaining* Cydaria *with courtship in dumb show.*

Vasq. Spain's mighty monarch, to whom heaven thinks fit, That all the nations of the earth submit, In gracious clemency, does condescend On these conditions to become your friend: First, that of him you shall your sceptre hold; Next, you present him with your useless gold ; Last, that you leave those idols you implore And one true Deity with him adore.

Mont. You speak your prince a mighty emperor, But his demands have spoke him proud and poor: He proudly at my free-born sceptre flies, Yet poorly begs a metal I despise. Gold thou mayest take, whatever thou canst find, Save what for sacred uses is designed: But, by what right pretends your king to be The sovereign lord of all the world and me?

Piz. The sovereign priest—— Who represents on earth the power of heaven, Has this your empire to our monarch given.

Mont. Ill does he represent the powers above, Who nourishes debate, not preaches love;

Besides, what greater folly can be shown? He gives another what is not his own.

Vasq. His power must needs unquestioned be below, For he in heaven an empire can bestow.

Mont. Empires in heaven he with more ease may give, And you, perhaps, would with less thanks receive: But heaven has need of no such viceroy here, Itself bestows the crowns that monarchs wear.

Piz. You wrong his power, as you mistake our end, Who came thus far religion to extend.

Mont. He, who religion truly understands, Knows its extent must be in men, not lands.

Odm. But who are those that truth must propagate Within the confines of my father's state?

Vasq. Religious men, who hither must be sent As awful guides of heavenly government; To teach you penance, fasts, and abstinence, To punish bodies for the soul's offence.

Mont. Cheaply you sin, and punish crimes with ease, Not as the offended, but the offenders please; First injure heaven, and, when its wrath is due, Yourselves prescribe it how to punish you.

Odm. What numbers of these holy men must come?

Piz. You shall not want, each village shall have some; Who, though the royal dignity they own, Are equal to it, and depend on none.

Guy. Depend on none! you treat them sure in state, For 'tis their plenty does their pride create.

Mont. Those ghostly kings would parcel out my power, And all the fatness of my land devour. That monarch sits not safely on his throne Who bears, within, a power that shocks his own. They teach obedience to imperial sway, But think it sin if they themselves obey.

Vasq. It seems, then, our religion you accuse, And peaceful homage to our king refuse?

Mont. Your Gods I slight not, but will keep my own; My crown is absolute, and holds of none. I cannot in a base subjection live, Nor suffer you to take, though I would give.

Cort. Is this your answer, sir?

Mont. ——This, as a prince, Bound to my people's and my crown's defence, I must return; but, as a man, by you Redeemed from death, all gratitude is due.

Cort. It was an act my honour bound me to: But what I did, were I again to do, I could not do it on my honour's score, For love would now oblige me to do more. Is no way left that we may yet agree? Must I have war, yet have no enemy?

Vasq. He has refused all terms of peace to take.

Mont. Since we must fight, hear, heavens, what prayers I make! First, to preserve this ancient state and me, But if your doom the fall of both decree, Grant only he, who has such honour shown, When I am dust, may fill my empty throne!

Cort. To make me happier than that wish can do, Lies not in all your Gods to grant, but you; Let this fair princess but one minute stay, A look from her will your obligements pay.

[*Exeunt* Montezuma, Odmar, Guyomar, Orbellan, Almeria, *and* Alibech.

Mont, to *Cyd.* Your duty in your quick return be shown—— Stay you, and wait my daughter to the town.

[*To his guards.*

[Cydaria *is going, but turns and looks back upon* Cortez, *who is looking on her all this while.*

Cyd. My father's gone, and yet I cannot go; Sure I have something lost or left behind!

[*Aside.*

Cort. Like travellers who wander in the snow, I on her beauty gaze 'till I am blind.

[*Aside.*

Cyd. Thick breath, quick pulse, and heaving of my heart, All signs of some unwonted change appear: I find myself unwilling to depart, And yet I know not why I would be here. Stranger, you raise such torments in my breast, That when I go (if I must go again), I'll tell my father you have robbed my rest, And to him of your injuries complain.

Cort. Unknown, I swear, those wrongs were which I wrought, But my complaints will much more just appear, Who from another world my freedom brought, And to your conquering eyes have lost it here.

Cyd. Where is that other world, from whence you came?

Cort. Beyond the ocean, far from hence it lies.

Cyd. Your other world, I fear, is then the same, That souls must go to when the body dies. But what's the cause that keeps you here with me, That I may know what keeps me here with you?

Cort. Mine is a love which must perpetual be, If you can be so just as I am true.

{{center|*Enter* Orbellan.

Orb. Your father wonders much at your delay.

Cyd. So great a wonder for so small a stay!

Orb. He has commanded you with me to go.

Cyd. Has he not sent to bring the stranger too?

Orb. If he to-morrow dares in fight appear, His high-placed love perhaps may cost him dear.

Cort. Dares!—— That word was never spoke to Spaniard yet, But forfeited his life, that gave him it; Haste quickly with thy pledge of safety hence, Thy guilt's protected by her innocence.

Cyd. Sure in some fatal hour my love was born, So soon o'ercast with absence in the morn !

Cort. Turn hence those pointed glories of your eyes; For if more charms beneath those circles rise, So weak my virtue, they so strong appear, I shall turn ravisher to keep you here.

[*Exeunt omnes.*

<poem>

ACT II.

SCENE I.—*The Magicians Cave.*

Enter Montezuma, *and High-Priest.*

Mont. Not that I fear the utmost fate can do, Come I the event of doubtful war to know; For life and death are things indifferent; Each to be chose as either brings content: My motive from a nobler cause does spring, Love rules my heart, and is your monarch's king; I more desire to know Almeria's mind, Than all that heaven has for my state designed.

High Pr. By powerful charms, which nothing can withstand, I'll force the gods to tell what you demand.

charm.

Thou moon, that aidst us with thy magic might, And ye small stars, the scattered seeds of light, Dart your pale beams into this gloomy place, That the sad powers of the infernal race May read above what's hid from human eyes, And in your walks see empires fall and rise. And ye, immortal souls, that once were men, And now, resolved to elements again, That wait for mortal frames in depths below, And did before what we are doomed to do ; Once, twice, and thrice, I wave my sacred wand, Ascend, ascend, ascend at my command.

[*An earthy spirit rises.*

Spir. In vain, O mortal men, your prayers implore The aid of powers below, that want it more; A God more strong, who all the Gods commands, Drives us to exile from our native lands; The air swarms thick with wandering deities, Which drowsily, like humming beetles, rise From our loved earth, where peacefully we slept, And, far from heaven, a long possession kept The frighted satyrs, that in woods delight, Now into plains with pricked-up ears take flight; And scudding thence, while they their horn-feet ply, About their sires the little silvans cry. A nation loving gold must rule this place, Our temples ruin, and our rites deface: To them, O king, is thy lost sceptre given. Now mourn thy fatal search, for since wise heaven More ill than good to mortals does dispense, It is not safe to have too quick a sense.

[*Descends.*

Mont. Mourn they, who think repining can remove The firm decrees of those that rule above; The brave are safe within, who still dare die: Whene'er I fall, I'll scorn my destiny. Doom as they please my empire not to stand, I'll grasp my sceptre with my dying hand.

High Pr. Those earthy spirits black and envious are; I'll call up other gods, of form more fair: Who visions dress in pleasing colour still, Set all the good to show, and hide the ill . Kalib, ascend, my fair-spoke servant rise, And sooth my heart with pleasing prophecies.

Kalib ascends all in white, in shape of a woman, and sings.

Kal. I looked and saw within the book of fate, Where many days did lowr, When lo ! one happy hour   Leapt up, and smiled to save thy sinking state;

A day shall come when in thy power Thy cruel foes shall be; Then shall thii land be free, And thou in peace shalt reign.   But take, O take that opportunity, Which, once refused, wilt never come again.

[*Descends.*

Mont. I shall deserve my fate, if I refuse That happy hour which heaven allots to use: But of my crown thou too much care dost take; That which I value more, my love's at stake.

High Pr. Arise, ye subtle spirits, that can spy, When love is entered in a female's eye; You, that can read it in the midst of doubt, And in the midst of frowns can find it out; You, that can search those many cornered minds, Where women's crooked fancy turns and winds; You, that can love explore, and truth impart, Where both lie deepest hid in woman's heart, Arise——

——

[*The ghosts of* Traxalla *and* Acacis *arise; they stand still, and point at* Montezuma.

High Pr. I did not for these ghastly visions send; Their sudden coming does some ill portend. Begone—begone—they will not disappear! My soul is seized with an unusual fear.

Mont. Point on, point on, and see whom you can fright. Shame and confusion seize these shades of night! Ye thin and empty forms, am I your sport?

[*They smile.*

If you were flesh—— You know you durst not use me in this sort.

[*The ghost of the Indian Queen rises betwixt the ghosts, with a dagger in her breast.*

Mont. Ha! I feel my hair grow stiff, my eyeballs roll! This is the only form could shake my soul.

Ghost. The hopes of thy successless love resign; Know, Montezuma, thou art only mine; For those, that here on earth their passion show By death for love, receive their right below. Why dost thou then delay my longing arms? Have cares, and age, and mortal life such charms? The moon grows sickly at the sight of day, And early cocks have summoned me away; Yet I'll appoint a meeting-place below, For there fierce winds o'er dusky valleys blow, Whose every puff bears empty shades away, Which guideless in those dark dominions stray. Just at the entrance of the fields below, Thou shalt behold a tall black poplar grow; Safe in its hollow trunk I will attend, And seize thy spirit when thou dost descend.

[*Descends.*

Mont. I'll seize thee there, thou messenger of fate. Would my short life had yet a shorter date! I 'm weary of this flesh which holds us here, And dastards manly souls with hope and fear; These heats and colds still in our breast make war, Agues and fevers all our passions are.

[*Exeunt.*

SCENE II.

Cydaria *and* Alibech, *betwixt the two armies.*

Alib. Blessings will crown your name, if you prevent That blood, which in this battle will be spent; Nor need you fear so just a suit to move, Which both becomes your duty and your love.

Cyd. But think you he will come? their camp is near, And he already knows I wait him here.

Alib. You are too young your power to understand, Lovers take wing upon the least command; Already he is here.

Enter Cortez *and* Vasquez *to them.*

Cort. Methinks, like two black storms on either hand, Our Spanish army and your Indians stand; This only space betwixt the clouds is clear, While you, like day, broke loose from both appear.

Cyd. Those closing skies might still continue bright, But who can help it, if you'll make it night? The gods have given you power of life and death, Like them to save, or scatter with a breath.

Cort. That power they to your father did dispose, 'Twas in his choice to make us friends or foes.

Alib. Injurious strength would rapine still excuse, By offering terms the weaker must refuse; And such as these your hard conditions are, You threaten peace, and you invite a war.

Cort. If for myself to conquer here I came, You might perhaps my actions justly blame: Now I am sent, and am not to dispute My prince's orders, but to execute.

Alib. He, who his prince so blindly does obey, To keep his faith his virtue throws away.

Cort. Monarchs may err; but should each private breast Judge their ill acts, they would dispute their best.

Cyd. Then all your care is for your prince, I see; Your truth to him outweighs your love to me: You may so cruel to deny me prove, But never after that pretend to love.

Cort. Command my life, and I will soon obey; To save my honour I my blood will pay.

Cyd. What is this honour which does love control?

Cort. A raging fit of virtue in the soul; A painful burden which great minds must bear, Obtained with danger, and possest with fear.

Cyd. Lay down that burden if it painful grow; You'll find, without it, love will lighter go.

Cort. Honour, once lost, is never to be found.

Alib. Perhaps he looks to have both passions crowned; First dye his honour in a purple flood, Then court the daughter in the father's blood.

Cort. The edge of war I 'll from the battle take, And spare her father's subjects for her sake.

Cyd. I cannot love you less when I 'm refused, But I can die to be unkindly used; Where shall a maid's distracted heart find rest, If she can miss it in her lover's breast ?

Cort. I till to-morrow will the fight delay; Remember you have conquered me to-day.

Alib. This grant destroys all you have urged before; Honour could not give this, or can give more. Our women in the foremost ranks appear; March to the fight, and meet your mistress there: Into the thickest squadrons she must run, Kill her, and see what honour will be won.

Cyd. I must be in the battle, but I 'll go With empty quiver and unbended bow; Not draw an arrow in this fatal strife, For fear its point should reach your noble life.

Enter Pizarro.

Cort. No more: your kindness wounds me to the death: Honour, be gone! what art thou but a breath? I'll live, proud of my infamy and shame, Graced with no triumph but a lover's name; Men can but say, love did his reason blind, And love's the noblest frailty of the mind.— Draw off my men; the war's already done.

Piz. Your orders come too late, the fight's begun; The enemy gives on, with fury led, And fierce Orbellan combats at their head.

Cort. He justly fears, a peace with me would prove Of ill concernment to his haughty love; Retire, fair excellence ! I go to meet New honour, but to lay it at your feet

[*Exeunt* Cortez, Vasquez, *and* Pizarro.

Enter Odmar *and* Guyomar, *to* Alibech *and* Cydaria.

Odm. Now, madam, since a danger does appear Worthy my courage, though below my fear; Give leave to him, who may in battle die, Before his death, to ask his destiny.

Guy. He cannot die, whom you command to live; Before the fight, you can the conquest give; Speak, where you 'll place it?

Alib. Briefly, then, to both, One I in secret love, the other loathe; But where I hate, my hate I will not show, And he, I love, my love shall never know; True worth shall gain me, that it may be said, Desert, not fancy, once a woman led. He who, in fight, his courage shall oppose, With most success, against his country's foes, From me shall all that recompence receive, That valour merits, or that love can give. 'Tis true my hopes and fears are all for one, But hopes and fears are to myself alone. Let him not shun the danger of the strife ; I but his love, his country claims his life.

Odm. All obstacles my courage shall remove.

Guy. Fall on, fall on.

Odm. For liberty!

Guy. For love!

[*Exeunt, the women following.*

<poem>

SCENE III.—*Changes to the Indian country.*

Enter Montezuma, attended by the Indians.

Mont. Charge, charge! their ground the faint Traxallans yield! Bold in close ambush, base in open field. The envious devil did my fortune wrong:— Thus fought, thus conquered I when I was young.

[*Exit.*

Alarm. Enter Cortez *bloody.*

Cort. Furies pursue these false Traxallans' flight; Dare they be friends to us, and dare not fight? What friends can cowards be, what hopes appear Of help from such, who, where they hate, show fear!

Enter Pizarro *and* Vasquez.

Piz. The field grows thin; and those, that now remain, Appear but like the shadows of the slain.

Vasq. The fierce old king is vanished from the place, And in a cloud of dust, pursues the chase.

Cort. Their eager chase disordered does appear, Command our horse to charge them in the rear:

[*To* Pizarro.

You to our old Castilian foot retire,

[*To* Vasq.

Who yet stand firm, and at their backs give fire.

[*Exeunt severally.*

SCENE IV.

Enter Odmar *and* Guyomar, *meeting each other in the battle.*

Odm. Where hast thou been, since first the fight began, Thou less than woman in the shape of man?

Guy. Where I have done what may thy envy move, Things worthy of my birth, and of my love.

Odm. Two bold Traxallans with one dart I slew, And left it sticking ere my sword I drew.

Guy. I sought not honour on so base a train, Such cowards by our women may be slain; I felled along a man of bearded face, His limbs all covered with a shining case: So wondrous hard, and so secure of wound, It made my sword though edged with flint, rebound.

Odm. I killed a double man; the one half lay Upon the ground, the other ran away.

[*Guns go off within.*

Enter Montezuma, *out of breath, with him* Alibech, *and an Indian.*

Mont. All's lost!— Our foes with lightning and with thunder fight; My men in vain shun death by shameful flight: For deaths invisible come winged with fire, They hear a dreadful noise, and straight expire. Take, gods! that soul, ye did in spite create, And made it great, to be unfortunate: Ill fate for me unjustly you provide, Great souls are sparks of your own heavenly pride: That lust of power we from your god-heads have, You 're bound to please those appetites you gave.

Enter Vasquez *and* Pizarro, *with Spaniards.*

Vasq. Pizarro, I have hunted hard to-day, Into our toils, the noblest of the prey; Seize on the king, and him your prisoner make, While I, in kind revenge, my taker take.

[Pizarro, *with two, goes to attack the king.* Vasquez, *with another, to seize* Alibech.

Guy. Their danger is alike;—whom shall I free?

Odm. I'll follow love!

Guy. I'll follow piety!

[Odmar *retreats from* Vasquez, *with* Alibech, *off the stage;* Guyomar *fights for his father.*

Guy. Fly, sir! while I give back that life you gave; Mine is well lost, if I your life can save.

[Montezuma *fights off;* Guyomar, *making his retreat, stays.*

Guy. 'Tis more than man can do to scape them all; Stay, let me see where noblest I may fall.

[*He runs at* Vasquez, *is seized behind and taken.*

Vasq. Conduct him off, And give command, he strictly guarded be.

Guy. In vain are guards, death sets the valiant free.

[*Exit* Guyomar, *with guards.*

Vasq. A glorious day! and bravely was it fought: Great fame our general in great dangers sought; From his strong arm I saw his rival run, And, in a crowd, the unequal combat shun.
Enter Cortez *leading* Cydaria, *who seems crying and begging of him.*

Cort. Man's force is fruitless, and your gods would fail To save the city, but your tears prevail; I'll of my fortune no advantage make, Those terms, they had once given, they still may take.

Cyd. Heaven has of right all victory designed, Where boundless power dwells in a will confined; Your Spanish honour does the world excel.

Cort. Our greatest honour is in loving well.

Cyd. Strange ways you practise there, to win a heart; Here love is nature, but with you 'tis art

Cort. Love is with us as natural as here, But fettered up with customs more severe. In tedious courtship we declare our pain, And, ere we kindness find, first meet disdain.

Cyd. If women love, they needless pains endure; Their pride and folly but delay their cure.

Cort. What you miscall their folly, is their care; They know how fickle common lovers are: Their oaths and vows are cautiously believed, For few there are but have been once deceived.

Cyd. But if they are not trusted when they vow, What other marks of passion can they show?

Cort. With feasts, and music, all that brings delight, Men treat their ears, their palates, and their sight

Cyd. Your gallants, sure, have little eloquence, Failing to move the soul, they court the sense: With pomp, and trains, and in a crowd they woo, When true felicity is but in two; But can such toys your women's passions move? This is but noise and tumult, 'tis not love.

Cort. I have no reason, madam, to excuse Those ways of gallantry, I did not use; My love was true, and on a nobler score.

Cyd. Your love, alas! then have you loved before?

Cort. 'Tis true I loved, but she is dead, she's dead; And I should think with her all beauty fled, Did not her fair resemblance live in you, And, by that image, my first flames renew.

Cyd. Ah! happy beauty, whosoe'er thou art! Though dead, thou keep'st possession of his heart; Thou mak'st me jealous to the last degree, And art my rival in his memory: Within his memory! ah, more than so, Thou liv'st and triumph'st o'er Cydaria too.

Cort. What strange disquiet has uncalmed your breast, Inhuman fair, to rob the dead of rest!— Poor heart! she slumbers in her silent tomb; Let her possess in peace that narrow room.

Cyd. Poor heart!—he pities and bewails her death!— Some god, much hated soul, restore thy breath, That I may kill thee; but, some ease 'twill be, I'll kill myself for but resembling thee.

Cort. I dread your anger, your disquiet fear, But blows, from hands so soft, who would not bear? So kind a passion why should I remove? Since jealousy but shows how well we love. Yet jealousy so strange I never knew; Can she, who loves me not, disquiet you? For in the grave no passions fill the breast, 'Tis all we gain by death, to be at rest

Cyd. That she no longer loves, brings no relief; Your love to her still lives, and that's my grief.

Cort. The object of desire once ta'en away, 'Tis then not love, but pity, that we pay.

Cyd. 'Tis such a pity I should never have, When I must lie forgotten in the grave; I meant to have obliged you, when I died, That, after me, you should love none beside.— But you are false already.

Cort. If untrue, By heaven! my falsehood is to her, not you.

Cyd. Observe, sweet heaven, how falsely he does swear!— You said, you loved me for resembling her.

Cort. That love was in me by resemblance bred, But shows you cheered my sorrows for the dead.

Cyd. You still repeat the greatness of your grief!

Cort. If that was great, how great was the relief.

Cyd. The first love still the strongest we account.

Cort. That seems more strong which could the first surmount: But if you still continue thus unkind, Whom I love best, you, by my death, shall find.

Cyd. If you should die, my death shall yours pursue; But yet I am not satisfied you're true.

Cort. Hear me, ye gods! and punish him you hear, If aught within the world I hold so dear.

Cyd. You would deceive the gods and me; she's dead, And is not in the world, whose love I dread.— Name not the world; say, nothing is so dear.

Cort. Then nothing is,—let that secure your fear.

Cyd. Tis time must wear it off, but I must go. Can you your constancy in absence show?

Cort. Misdoubt my constancy, and do not try, But stay, and keep me ever in your eye.

Cyd. If as a prisoner I were here, you might Have then insisted on a conqueror's right, And stayed me here; but now my love would be The effect of force, and I would give it free.

Cort. To doubt your virtue, or your love, were sin! Call for the captive prince, and bring him in.

Enter Guyomar, *bound and sad.*

You look, sir, as your fate you could not bear:

[*To* Guy.

Are Spanish fetters, then, so hard to wear? Fortune's unjust, she ruins oft the brave, And him, who should be victor, makes the slave.

Guy. Son of the sun! my fetters cannot be But glorious for me, since put on by thee: The ills of love, not those of fate, I fear; These can I brave, but those I cannot bear: My rival brother, while I 'm held in chains, In freedom reaps the fruit of all my pains.

Cort. Let it be never said that he, whose breast Is filled with love, should break a lover's rest— Haste! lose no time!—your sister sets you free:— And tell the king, my generous enemy, I offer still those terms he had before, Only ask leave his daughter to adore.

Guy. Brother, (that name my breast shall ever own,

[*He embraces him.*

The name of foe be but in battles known;) For some few days all hostile acts forbear, That, if the king consents, it seem not fear: His heart is noble, and great souls must be Most sought and courted in adversity.— Three days, I hope, the wished success will tell.

    Cyd. Till that long time,

    Cort. Till that long time, farewell.

                                                          [Exeunt severally.

ACT III.

SCENE I.—*A Chamber Royal.*

Enter Odmar *and* Alibech.

Odm. The gods, fair Alibech, had so decreed, Nor could my valour against fate succeed; Yet though our army brought not conquest home, I did not from the fight inglorious come: If, as a victor, you the brave regard, Successless courage, then, may hope reward; And I, returning safe, may justly boast To win the prize which my dear brother lost.
Enter Guyomar *behind him.*

Guy. No, no, thy brother lives! and lives to be A witness, both against himself and thee; Though both in safety are returned again, I blush to ask her love for vanquished men.
Odm. Brother, I'll not dispute but you are brave; Yet I was free, and you, it seems, a slave.
Guy. Odmar, 'tis true that I was captive led; As publicly 'tis known, as that you fled: But of two shames, if she must one partake, I think the choice will not be hard to make.
Odm. Freedom and bondage in her choice remain; Darest thou expect she will put on thy chain ?
Guy. No, no, fair Alibech, give him the crown, My brother is returned with high renown: He thinks by flight his mistress must be won, And claims the prize, because he best did run.
Alib. Your chains were glorious, and your flight was wise, But neither have o'ercome your enemies: My secret wishes would my choice decide, But open justice bends to neither side.
Odm. Justice already does my right approve, If him, who loves you most, you most should love. My brother poorly from your aid withdrew, But I my father left, to succour you.
Guy. Her country she did to herself prefer, Him who fought best, not who defended her; Since she her interest, for the nation's waved, Then I, who saved the king, the nation saved. You, aiding her, your country did betray: I, aiding him, did her commands obey.
Odm. Name it no more; in love there is a time When dull obedience is the greatest crime. She to her country's use resigned your sword, And you, kind lover, took her at her word; You did your duty to your love prefer, Seek your reward from duty, not from her.
Guy. In acting what my duty did require, 'Twas hard for me to quit my own desire; That fought for her, which, when I did subdue, 'Twas much the easier task I left to you.
Alib. Odmar a more than common love has shown, And Guyomar's was greater, or was none; Which I should choose, some god direct my breast, The certain good, or the uncertain best— I cannot choose,—you both dispute in vain,— Time and your future acts must make it plain; First raise the siege, and set your country free, I, not the judge, but the reward, will be.
To them, Enter Montezuma, *talking with* Almeria *and* Orbellan.

Mont. Madam, I think, with reason, I extol The virtue of the Spanish general; When all the gods our ruin have foretold, Yet generously he does his arms withhold, And, offering peace, the first conditions make.

Alm. When peace is offered, 'tis too late to take; For one poor loss, to stoop to terms like those!— Were we o'ercome, what could they worse impose? Go, go, with homage your proud victors meet! Go, lie like dogs beneath your master's feet! Go, and beget them slaves to dig their mines, And groan for gold, which now in temples shines! Your shameful story shall record of me, The men all crouched, and left a woman free!

Guy. Had I not fought, or durst not fight again, I my suspected counsel should refrain: For I wish peace, and any terms prefer, Before the last extremities of war. We but exasperate those we cannot harm, And fighting gains us but to die more warm: If that be cowardice, which dares not see The insolent effects of victory, The rape of matrons, and their children's cries,— Then I am fearful, let the brave advise.

Odm. Keen cutting swords, and engines killing far, Have prosperously begun a doubtful war: But now our foes with less advantage fight, Their strength decreases with our Indians' fright

Mont. This noble vote does with my wish comply, I am for war.

Alm. And so am I.

Orb. And I.

Mont. Then send to break the truce, and I'll take care To cheer the soldiers, and for fight prepare.

[*Exeunt* Mont. Odm. Guy. *and* Alib.

Alm. to *Orb.* 'Tis now the hour which all to rest allow, And sleep sits heavy upon every brow; In this dark silence softly leave the town,

[Guyomar *returns, and hears them.*

And to the general's tent,—'tis quickly known,— Direct your steps: You may despatch him straight, Drowned in his sleep, and easy for his fate: Besides, the truce will make the guards more slack.

Orb. Courage, which leads me on, will bring me back.— But I more fear the baseness of the thing: Remorse, you know, bears a perpetual sting.

Alm. For mean remorse no room the valiant finds, Repentance is the virtue of weak minds; For want of judgment keeps them doubtful still, They may repent of good, who can of ill; But daring courage makes ill actions good, 'Tis foolish pity spares a rival's blood ; You shall about it straight.

[*Exeunt* Alm. *and* Orb.

Guy. Would they betray His sleeping virtue, by so mean a way!— And yet this Spaniard is our nation's foe,— I wish him dead,—but cannot wish it so;— Either my country never must be freed, Or I consenting to so black a deed.— Would chance had never led my steps this way! Now if he dies, I murder him, not they;— Something must be resolved ere 'tis too late;— He gave me freedom, I'll prevent his fate.

[*Exit.*

<poem>

SCENE II.—*A camp.*

Enter Cortez *alone, in a night-gown.*

Cort. All things are hushed, as nature's self lay dead; The mountains seem to nod their drowsy head; The little birds in dreams their songs repeat, And sleeping flowers beneath the night-dew sweat, Even lust and envy sleep; yet love denies Rest to my soul, and slumber to my eyes. Three days I promised to attend my doom, And two long days and nights are yet to come:— 'Tis sure the noise of some tumultuous fight,

[*Noise within.*

They break the truce and sally out by night.
Enter Orbellan, *flying in the dark, his sword drawn.*

Orb. Betrayed! pursued! O, whither shall I fly? See, see! the just reward of treachery!— I'm sure among the tents, but know not where; Even night wants darkness to secure my fear.

[*Comes near* Cortez, *who hears him.*

Cort. Stand! who goes there?
Orb. Alas, what shall I say?—

[*Aside.*

A poor Traxallan that mistook his way, And wanders in the terrors of the night
Cort. Soldier, thou seem'st afraid; whence comes thy flight?
Orb. The insolence of Spaniards caused my fear, Who in the dark pursued me entering here.
Cort. Their crimes shall meet immediate punishment, But stay thou safe within the general's tent
Orb. Still worse and worse.
Cort. Fear not, but follow me; Upon my life I'll set thee safe and free.

[Cortez *leads him in and returns.*

To him Vasquez, Pizarro, *and Spaniards with Torches.*

Vasq. O sir, thank heaven, and your brave Indian friend, That you are safe; Orbellan did intend This night to kill you sleeping in your tent: But Guyomar his trusty slave has sent, Who, following close his silent steps by night, Till in our camp they both approached the light Cried— Seize the traitor, seize the murderer ? The cruel villain fled I know not where; But far he is not, for he this way bent.
Piz. The enraged soldiers seek, from tent to tent, With lighted torches, and in love to you, With bloody vows his hated life pursue.
Vasq. This messenger does, since he came, relate, That the old king, after a long debate, By his imperious mistress blindly led, Has given Cydaria to Orbellan's bed.
Cort. Vasquez, the trusty slave with you retain; Retire a while, I'll call you back again.

[*Exeunt* Vasq. *and* Piz.

Cortez *at his tent door.*

Indian, come forth ; your enemies are gone, And I, who saved you from them, here alone.
Enter Orbellan, *holding his face aside.*

You hide your face, as you were still afraid: Dare you not look on him who gave you aid?

Orb. Moon, slip behind some cloud, some tempest, rise, And blow out all the stars that light the skies, To shroud my shame!

Cort. In vain you turn aside, And hide your face; your name you cannot hide: I know my rival and his black design.

Orb. Forgive it, as my passion's fault, not mine.

Cort. In your excuse your love does little say; You might, howe'er, have took a fairer way.

Orb. 'Tis true, my passion small defence can make; Yet you must spare me for your honour's sake, That was engaged to set me safe and free.

Cort. 'Twas to a stranger, not an enemy: Nor is it prudence to prolong thy breath, When all my hopes depend upon thy death; Yet none shall tax me with base perjury: Something I'll do, both for myself and thee; With vowed revenge my soldiers search each tent, If thou art seen, none can thy death prevent; Follow my steps with silence and with haste.

SCENE III.

They go out, the Scene changes to the Indian Country, they return.

Cort. Now you are safe, you have my outguards past.

Orb. Then here I take my leave.

Cort. Orbellan, no; When you return, you to Cydaria go; I'll send a message.

Orb. Let it be exprest; I am in haste.

Cort. I'll write it in your breast

[*Draws.*

Orb. What means my rival?

Cort. Either fight or die, I'll not strain honour to a point too high; I saved your life, and keep it if you can, Cydaria shall be for the bravest man; On equal terms you shall your fortune try, Take this, and lay your flint-edged weapon by;

[*Gives him a sword.*

I'll arm you for my glory, and pursue No palm, but what's to manly virtue due. Fame, with my conquest, shall my courage tell, This you shall gain, by placing love so well.

Orb. Fighting with you, ungrateful I appear.

Cort. Under that shadow, thou wouldst hide thy fear: Thou wouldst possess thy love at thy return, And in her arms my easy virtue scorn.

Orb. Since we must fight, no longer let's delay; The moon shines clear and makes a paler day.

[*They fight,* Orbellan *is wounded in the hand, his sword falls out of it.*

Cort. To courage, even of foes, there's pity due; It was not I, but fortune, vanquished you:

[*Throws his sword again.*

Thank me with that, and so dispute the prize, As if you fought before Cydaria's eyes.

Orb. I would not poorly such a gift requite; You gave me not this sword to yield, but fight:

[*He strives to hold it, but cannot.*

But see, where yours has forced its bloody way; My wounded hand my heart does ill obey.

Cort. Unlucky honour, that control'st my will! Why have I vanquished, since I must not kill? Fate sees thy life lodged in a brittle glass, And looks it through, but to it cannot pass.

Orb. All I can do is frankly to confess,— I wish I could, but cannot, love her less: To swear I would resign her, were but vain, Love would recall that perjured breath again; And in my wretched case, 'twill be more just, Not to have promised, than deceive your trust Know, if I live once more to see the town, In bright Cydaria's arms my love I'll crown.

Cort. In spite of that, I give thee liberty, And with thy person leave thy honour free; But to thy wishes move a speedy pace, Or death will soon o'ertake thee in the chase.— To arms, to arms; fate shows my love the way, I'll force the city on thy nuptial day.

Exeunt severally.

SCENE IV.—*Mexico.*

Enter Montezuma, Odmar, Guyomar, Almeria.

Mont. It moves my wonder that in two days' space, This early famine spreads so swift a pace.

Odm. 'Tis, sir, the general cry; nor seems it strange, The face of plenty should so swiftly change: This city never felt a siege before, But from the lake received its daily store; Which now shut up, and millions crowded here, Famine will soon in multitudes appear.

Mont. The more the number, still the greater shame.

Alm. What if some one should seek immortal fame, By ending of the siege at one brave blow ?

Mont. That were too happy!

Alm. Yet it may be so. What if the Spanish general should be slain?

Guy. Just heaven, I hope, does otherwise ordain.

Aside.

Mont. If slain by treason, I lament his death.
                    Enter Orbeixan, *and whispers his sister.*

Odm. Orbellan seems in haste, and out of breath.

Mont. Orbellan, welcome; you are early here, A bridegroom's haste does in your looks appear.

[Almeria *aside to her brother.*

Alm. Betrayed! no, 'twas thy cowardice and fear; He had not 'scaped with life, had I been there: But since so ill you act a brave design, Keep close your shame;—fate makes the next turn mine,
                    Enter Alibech *and* Cydaria.

Alib. O, sir, if ever pity touched your breast, Let it be now to your own blood exprest: In tears your beauteous daughter drowns her sight, Silent as dews that fall in dead of night.

Cyd. To your commands I strict obedience owe, And my last act of it I come to show: I want the heart to die before your eyes, But grief will finish that which fear denies.

Aim. Your will should by your father's precept move.

Cyd. When he was young, he taught me truth in love.

Aim. He found more love than he deserved, 'tis true, And that, it seems, is lucky too to you; Your father's folly took a headstrong course, But I'll rule yours, and teach you love by force.
                    Enter Messenger.

Mess. Arm, arm, O king! the enemy comes on, A sharp assault already is begun; Their murdering guns play fiercely on the walls.

Odm. Now, rival, let us run where honour calls.

Guy. I have discharged what gratitude did owe, And the brave Spaniard is again my foe.

[*Exeunt* Odmar *and* Guyomar.

Mont. Our walls are high, and multitudes defend: Their vain attempt must in their ruin end; The nuptials with my presence shall be graced.

Alib. At least but stay 'till the assault be past.

Alm. Sister, in vain you urge him to delay, The king has promised, and he shall obey.

Enter second Messenger.

2 *Mess.* From several parts the enemy's repelled, One only quarter to the assault does yield.

Enter third Messenger.

3 *Mess.* Some foes are entered, but they are so few, They only death, not victory, pursue.

Orb. Hark, hark, they shout! From virtue's rules I do too meanly swerve. I, by my courage, will your love deserve.

[*Exit.*

Mont. Here, in the heart of all the town, I 'll stay; And timely succour, where it wants, convey.

A noise within. Enter Orbellan, *Indians driven in,* Cortez *after them, and one or two Spaniards.*

Cort. He's found, he's found! degenerate coward, stay: Night saved thee once, thou shalt not 'scape by day.

[*Kills* Orbellan.

Orb. O, I am killed——

[*Dies.*

Enter Guyomar *and* Odmar.

Guy. Yield, generous stranger, and preserve your life; Why choose you death in this unequal strifc?

[*He is beset.*

[Almeria *and* Alibech *fall on* Orbellan's *body.*

Cort. What nobler fate could any lover meet? I fall revenged, and at my mistress' feet.

[*They fall on him, and bear him down;* Guyomar *takes his sword.*

Alib. He's past recovery; my dear brother's slain, Fate's hand was in it, and my care is vain.

Alm. In weak complaints you vainly waste your breath: They are not tears that can revenge his death. Despatch the villain straight.

Cort. The villain 's dead.

Alm. Give me a sword, and let me take his head.

Mont. Though, madam, for your brother's loss I grieve, Yet let me beg——

Alm. His murderer may live?

Cyd. 'Twas his misfortune, and the chance of war.

Cort. It was my purpose, and I killed him fair: How could you so unjust and cruel prove, To call that chance, which was the act of love?

Cyd. I called it anything to save your life: Would he were living still, and I his wife! That wish was once my greatest misery: But 'tis a greater to behold you die.

Alm. Either command his death upon the place, Or never more behold Almeria's face.

Guy. You by his valour once from death were freed: Can you forget so generous a deed?

[*To* Montezuma.

Mont. How gratitude and love divide my breast! Both ways alike my soul is robbed of rest. But—let him die—Can I his sentence give? Ungrateful, must he die, by whom I live? But can I then Almeria's tears deny? Should any live whom she commands to die?

Guy. Approach who dares: He yielded on my word; And, as my prisoner, I restore his sword.

[*Gives his sword.*

His life concerns the safety of the state, And I 'll preserve it for a calm debate.

Mont. Dar'st thou rebel, false and degenerate boy? That being, which I gave, I thus destroy. {{right[*Offers to kill him,* Odmar *steps between.*}}

Odm. My brother's blood I cannot see you spill. Since he prevents you but from doing ill. He is my rival, but his death would be For him too glorious, and too base for me.

Guy. Thou shalt not conquer in this noble strife: Alas, I meant not to defend my life: Strike, sir, you never pierced a breast more true; 'Tis the last wound I e'er can take for you. You see I live but to dispute your will: Kill me, and then you may my prisoner kill.

Cort. You shall not, generous youths, contend for me: It is enough that I your honour see: But that your duty may no blemish take, I will myself your father's captive make:

[*Gives his sword to* Montezuma.

When he dares strike, I am prepared to fall: The Spaniards will revenge their general.

Cyd. Ah, you too hastily your life resign, You more would love it, if you valued mine!

Cort. Despatch me quickly, I my death forgive; I shall grow tender else, and wish to live; Such an infectious face her sorrow wears, I can bear death, but not Cydaria's tears.

Alm. Make haste, make haste, they merit death all three: They for rebellion, and for murder he. See, see, my brother's ghost hangs hovering there O'er his warm blood, that steams into the air; Revenge, revenge, it cries.

Mont. And it shall have; But two days' respite for his life I crave: If in that space you not more gentle prove, I'll give a fatal proof how well I love. 'Till when, you, Guyomar, your prisoner take; Bestow him in the castle on the lake: In that small time I shall the conquest gain Of these few sparks of virtue which remain; Then all, who shall my headlong passion see, Shall curse my crimes, and yet shall pity me.

[*Exeunt.*

ACT IV.

SCENE I.—*A prison.*

Enter Almeria *and an Indian; they speak entering.*

Ind. A dangerous proof of my respect I show.
Alm. Fear not, Prince Guyomar shall never know: While he is absent let us not delay;
Remember 'tis the king thou dost obey.
Ind. See where he sleeps.

[Cortez *appears chained and laid asleep.*

Alm. Without, my coming wait; And, on thy life, secure the prison gate.

[*Exit Indian.*

[*She plucks out a dagger, and approaches him.*

Spaniard, awake: thy fatal hour is come: Thou shalt not at such ease receive thy doom.
Revenge is sure, though sometimes slowly paced; Awake, awake, or, sleeping, sleep thy last.
Cort. Who names revenge?
Alm. Look up, and thou shalt see.
Cort. I cannot fear so fair an enemy.
Alm. No aid is nigh, nor canst thou make defence: Whence can thy courage come?
Cort. From innocence.
Alm. From innocence? let that then take thy part Still are thy looks assured have at thy
heart !

[*Holds up the dagger.*

I cannot kill thee; sure thou bear'st some charm,

[*Goes back.*

Or some divinity holds back my arm. Why do I thus delay to make him bleed?

[*Aside.*

Can I want courage for so brave a deed? I Ve shook it off; my soul is free from fear.

[*Comes again.*

And I can now strike anywhere—but here: His scorn of death, how strangely does it
move! A mind so haughty who could choose but love!

[*Goes off.*

Plead not a charm, or any god's command, Alas, it is thy heart that holds thy hand: In
spite of me I love, and see, too late, My mother's pride must find my mother's fate. ——Thy

country's foe, thy brother's murderer,— For shame, Almeria, such mad thoughts forbear: It won'not be,—if I once more come on,

[Coming on again.

I shall mistake the breast, and pierce my own.

[Comes with her dagger down.

Cort. Does your revenge maliciously forbear To give me death, 'till 'tis prepared by fear? If you delay for that, forbear or strike, Foreseen and sudden death are both alike.

Alm. To show my love would but increase his pride: They have most power, who most their passions hide.

[Aside.

Spaniard, I must confess, I did expect You could not meet your death with such neglect; I will defer it now, and give you time: You may repent, and I forget your crime.

Cort. Those who repent acknowledge they do ill: I did not unprovoked your brother kill.

Alm. Petition me, perhaps I may forgive.

Cort. Who begs his life does not deserve to live.

Alm. But if 'tis given, you'll not refuse to take?

Cort. I can live gladly for Cydaria's sake.

Alm. Does she so wholly then possess your mind? What if you should another lady find, Equal to her in birth, and far above In all that can attract, or keep your love, Would you so doat upon your first desire, As not to entertain a nobler fire ?

Cort. I think that person hardly will be found, With gracious form and equal virtue crowned: Yet if another could precedence claim, My fixed desires could find no fairer aim.

Alm. Dull ignorance: he cannot yet conceive: To speak more plain, shame will not give me leave.

[Aside.

Suppose one loved you, whom even kings adore:

[To him.

Who, with your life, your freedom would restore, And add to that the crown of Mexico: Would you, for her, Cydaria's love forego?

Cort. Though she could offer all you can invent, I could not of my faith, once vowed, repent.

Alm. A burning blush has covered all my face; Why am I forced to publish my disgrace? What if I love? you know it cannot be, And yet I blush to put the case—'twere me. If I could love you with a flame so true, I could forget what hand my brother slew— —Make out the rest—I am disordered so, I know not further what to say or do: But answer me to what you think I meant.

Cort. Reason or wit no answer can invent: Of words confused who can the meaning find?

Alm. Disordered words show a distempered mind.

Cort. She has obliged me so, that could I choose, I would not answer what I must refuse.

[Aside.

Alm. His mind is shook——suppose I loved you, speak, Would you for me Cydaria's fetters break?

Cort. Things, meant in jest, no serious answer need.

Alm. But, put the case that it were so indeed.

Cort. If it were so,—which but to think were pride,— My constant love would dangerously be tried: For since you could a brother's death forgive, He whom you save, for you alone should live: But I, the most unhappy of mankind, Ere I knew yours, have all my love resigned: 'Tis my own loss I grieve, who have no more: You go a-begging to a bankrupt's door. Yet could I change, as sure I never can, How could you love so infamous a man? For love, once given from her, and placed in you, Would leave no ground I ever could be true.

Alm. You construed me aright—I was in jest: And, by that offer, meant to sound your breast; Which since I find so constant to your love, Will much my value of your worth improve. Spaniard, assure yourself you shall not be Obliged to quit Cydaria for me: 'Tis dangerous though to treat me in thi.s sort, And to refuse my offers, though in sport

[*Exit.*

Cort. In what a strange condition am I left? More than I wish I have, of all I wish bereft! In wishing nothing, we enjoy still most; For even our wish is, in possession, lost: Restless, we wander to a new desire, And burn ourselves, by blowing up the fire: We toss and turn about our feverish will, When all our ease must come by lying still: For all the happiness mankind can gain Is not in pleasure, but in rest from pain.

[*Goes in, and the scene closes upon him.*

<poem>

SCENE II.—*Chamber-royal.*

Enter Montezuma, Odmar, Guyomar, *and* Alibech.

Mont. My ears are deaf with this impatient crowd.

Odm. Their wants are now grown mutinous and loud: The general's taken, but the siege remains; And their last food our dying men sustains.

Guy. One means is only left. I to this hour Have kept the captive from Almeria's power; And though, by your command, she often sent To urge his doom, do still his death prevent.

Mont. That hope is past: Him I have oft assailed; But neither threats nor kindness have prevailed; Hiding our wants, I offered to release His chains, and equally conclude a peace: He fiercely answered, I had now no way But to submit, and without terms obey; I told him, he in chains demanded more Than he imposed in victory before: He sullenly replied, he could not make These offers now; honour must give, not take.

Odm. Twice have I sallied, and was twice beat back; What desp'rate course remains for us to take?

Mont. If either death or bondage I must choose, I'll keep my freedom, though my life I lose.

Guy. I'll not upbraid you, that you once refused Those means, you might have then with honour used; I'll lead your men, perhaps bring victory: They know to conquer best, who know to die.

[*Exeunt* Montezuma *and* Odmar.

Alib. Ah me, what have I heard! stay, Guyomar, What hope you from this sally you prepare?

Guy. A death, with honour, for my country's good: A death, to which yourself designed my blood.

Alib. You heard, and I well know the town's distress, Which sword and famine both at once oppress: Famine so fierce, that what's denied man's use, Even deadly plants, and herbs of poisonous juice, Wild hunger seeks; and, to prolong our breath, We greedily devour our certain death: The soldier in th' assault of famine falls: And ghosts, not men, are watching on the walls. As callow birds—— Whose mother's killed in seeking of the prey, Cry in their nest, and think her long away; And at each leaf that stirs, each blast of wind, Gape for the food, which they must never find: So cry the people in their misery.

Guy. And what relief can they expect from me?

Alib. While Montezuma sleeps, call in the foe: The captive general your design may know: His noble heart, to honour ever true, Knows how to spare as well as to subdue.

Guy. What I have heard I blush to hear: and grieve, Those words you spoke I must your words believe. I to do this! I, whom you once thought brave, To sell my country, and my king enslave? All I have done by one foul act deface, And yield my right to you, by turning base? What more could Odmar wish that I should do, To lose your love, than you persuade me to? No, madam, no, I never can commit A deed so ill, nor can you suffer it: 'Tis but to try what virtue you can find Lodged in my soul.

Alib. I plainly speak my mind; Dear as my life my virtue I 'll preserve, But virtue you too scrupulously serve: I loved not more than now my country's good, When for its service I employed your blood: But things are altered, I am still the same, By different ways still moving to one fame; And by disarming you, I now do more To save the town, than arming you before.

Guy. Things good or ill by circumstances be, In you 'tis virtue, what is vice in me.

Alib. That ill is pardoned, which does good procure.

Guy. The good's uncertain, but the ill is sure.

Alib. When kings grow stubborn, slothful, or unwise, Each private man for public good should rise. As when the head distempers does endure, Each several part must join to effect the cure.

Guy. Take heed, fair maid, how monarchs you accuse: Such reasons none but impious rebels use: Those, who to empire by dark paths aspire, Still plead a call to what they most desire; But kings by free consent their kingdoms take, Strict as those sacred ties which nuptials make; And whate'er faults in princes time reveal, None can be judge where can be no appeal.

Alib. In all debates you plainly let me see You love your virtue best, but Odmar me: Go, your mistaken piety pursue: I'll have from him what is denied by you; With my commands you shall no more be graced. Remember, sir, this trial was your last.

Guy. The gods inspire you with a better mind; Make you more just, and make you then more kind! But though from virtue's rules I cannot part, Think I deny you with a bleeding heart: 'Tis hard with me whatever choice I make; I must not merit you, or must forsake: But in this strait, to honour I 'll be true, And leave my fortune to the gods and you.

Enter Messenger privately.

Mess. Now is the time; be aiding to your fate; From the watch-tower, above the western gate, I have discerned the foe securely lie, Too proud to fear a beaten enemy: Their careless chiefs to the cool grottoes run, The bowers of kings, to shade them from the sun.

Guy. Upon thy life disclose thy news to none; I'll make the conquest or the shame my own. {{right|[*Exeunt* Guyomar} *and Messenger.*

Enter Odmar.

Alib. I read some welcome message in his eye: Prince Odmar comes: I1l see if he 'll deny.— Odmar, I come to tell you pleasing news; I begged a thing, your brother did refuse.

Odm. The news both pleases me, and grieves me too; For nothing, sure, should be denied to you: But he was blessed who might commanded be; You never meant that happiness to me.

'*Alib. What he refused, your kindness might bestow,* But my commands, perhaps, your burden grow.

Odm. Could I but live till burdensome they prove, My life would be immortal as my love. Your wish, ere it receive a name, I grant.

Alib. 'Tis to relieve your dying country's want; All hopes of succour from your arms is past, To save us now you must our ruin haste; Give up the town, and, to oblige him more, The captive general's liberty restore.

Odm. You speak to try my love; can you forgive So soon, to let your brother's murderer live?

Alib. Orbellan, though my brother, did disgrace, With treacherous deeds, our mighty mother's race; And to revenge his blood, so justly spilt, What is it less than to partake his guilt? Though my proud sister to revenge incline, I to my country's good my own resign.

Odm. To save our lives, our freedom I betray— Yet, since I promised it, I will obey; I 'll not my shame nor your commands dispute; You shall behold your empire 's absolute.

[*Exit.*

Alib. I should have thanked him for his speedy grant, And yet, I know not how, fit words I want: Sure I am grown distracted in my mind;— That joy, this grant should bring, I cannot find: The one, denying, vexed my soul before; And this, obeying, has disturbed me more: The one, with grief, and slowly, did refuse, The other, in his grant, much haste did use: —He used too much—and, granting me so soon, He has the merit of the gift undone: Methought with wondrous ease he swallowed down His forfeit honour, to betray the town: My inward choice was Guyomar before, But now his virtue has confirmed me more—— I rave, I rave, for Odmar will obey, And then my promise must my choice betray. Fantastic honour, thou hast framed a toil Thyself, to make thy love thy virtue's spoil.

[*Exit.*

SCENE III.

A pleasant grotto discovered; in it a fountain spouting; roundabout it Vasquez, Pizarro, *and other Spaniards, lying carelessly unarmed, and by them many Indian women, one of which sings the following song.*   song.

Ah fading joy! how quickly art thou past! Yet we thy ruin haste. As if the cares of human life were few, We seek out new: And follow fate, that does too fast pursue. See, how on every bough the birds express, In their sweet notes, their happiness. They all enjoy, and nothing spare; But on their mother nature lay their care: Why then should man, the lord of all below, Such troubles choose to know, As none of all his subjects undergo ? Hark, hark, the waters, fall, fall, fall, And with a murmuring sound Dash, dash, upon the ground, To gentle slumbers call. After the song two Spaniards arise, and dance a saraband with castanietas: At the end of which Guyomar *and his Indians enter, and, ere the Spaniards can recover their swords, seize them.*

Guy. Those, whom you took without, in triumph bring; But see these straight conducted to the king.

Piz. Vasquez, what now remains in these extremes?

Vasq. Only to wake us from our golden dreams.

Piz. Since by our shameful conduct we have lost Freedom, wealth, honour, which we value most, I wish they would our lives a period give: They live too long, who happiness outlive.

[*Spaniards are led out.*

1 Ind. See, sir, how quickly your success is spread; The king comes marching in the army's head.

Enter Montezuma, Alibech, Odmar *discontented.*

Mont. Now all the gods reward and bless my son.

[*Embracing.*

Thou hast this day thy father's youth outdone.

Alib. Just heaven all happiness upon him shower, Till it confess its will beyond its power.

Guy. The heavens are kind, the gods propitious be, I only doubt a mortal deity: I neither fought for conquest, nor for fame, Your love alone can recompense my flame.

Alib. I gave my love to the most brave in war; But that the king must judge.

Mont. ——'Tis Guyomar.

[*Soldiers shout,* A Guyomar, *etc.*

Mont. This day your nuptials we will celebrate; But guard these haughty captives till their fate: Odmar, this night to keep them be your care, To-morrow for their sacrifice prepare.

Alib. Blot not your conquest with your cruelty.

Mont. Fate says, we are not safe unless they die: The spirit, that foretold this happy day,

Bid me use caution and avoid delay: Posterity be juster to my fame ; Nor call it murder, when each private man In his defence may justly do the same: But private persons more than monarchs can : All weigh our acts, and whate'er seems unjust, Impute not to necessity, but lust

[*Exeunt* Montezuma, Guyomar, *and* Alibech.

Odm. Lost and undone! he had my father's voice, And Alibech seemed pleased with her new choice: Alas, it was not new! too late I see, Since one she hated, that it must be me. ——I feel a strange temptation in my will To do an action, great at once and ill: Virtue, ill treated, from my soul is fled; I by revenge and love am wholly led: Yet conscience would against my rage rebel—— —Conscience, the foolish pride of doing well ! Sink empire, father perish, brother fall, Revenge does more than recompense you all.— Conduct the prisoners in.

Enter Vasquez, *and* Pizarro.

Spaniards, you see your own deplored estate: What dare you do to reconcile your fate?

Vasq. All that despair, with courage joined, can do.

Odm. An easy way to victory I 'll show: When all are buried in their sleep or joy, Ill give you arms, burn, ravish, and destroy; For my own share one beauty I design;— Engage your honour that she shall be mine.

Piz. I gladly swear.

Vasq. ——And I; but I request That in return, one, who has touched my breast, Whose name I know not, may be given to me.

Odm. Spaniard, 'tis just; she's yours, whoe'er she be.

Vasq. The night comes on: if fortune bless the bold, I shall possess the beauty.

Piz. I the gold.

[*Exeunt.*

SCENE IV.—*A Prison.*

Cortez *discovered bound:* Almeria *talking with him.*

Alm. I come not now your constancy to prove; You may believe me when I say I love.
Cort. You have too well instructed me before In your intentions, to believe you more.
Alm. I'm justly plagued by this your unbelief, And am myself the cause of my own grief: But to beg love, I cannot stoop so low; It is enough that you my passion know: Tis in your choice; love me, or love me not; I have not yet my brother's death forgot.

[*Lays hold on the dagger.*

Cort. You menace me and court me in a breath: Your Cupid looks as dreadfully as death.
Alm. Your hopes, without, are vanished into smoke: Your captains taken, and your armies broke.
Cort. In vain you urge me with my miseries: When fortune falls, high courages can rise; Now should I change my love, it would appear Not the effect of gratitude, but fear.
Alm. I'll to the king, and make it my request, Or my command, that you may be releast; And make you judge, when I have set you free, Who best deserves your passion, I, or she.
Cort. You tempt my faith so generous a way, As without guilt might constancy betray: But I 'm so far from meriting esteem, That, if I judge, I must myself condemn; Yet having given my worthless heart before, What I must ne'er possess, I will adore: Take my devotion then this humbler way; Devotion is the love which heaven we pay.

[*Kisses her hand.*

Enter Cydaria.

Cyd. May I believe my eyes! what do I see! Is this her hate to him, his love to me! 'Tis in my breast she sheathes her dagger now. False man, is this thy faith? is this thy vow?

[*To him.*

Cort. What words, dear saint, are these I hear you use? What faith, what vows, are those which you accuse?
Cyd. More cruel than the tiger o'er his spoil; And falser than the weeping crocodile: Can you add vanity to guilt, and take A pride to hear the conquests, which you make? Go, publish your renown; let it be said, You have a woman, and that loved, betrayed.
Cort. With what injustice is my faith accused! Life, freedom, empire, I at once refused; And would again ten thousand times for you.
Alm. She'll have too great content to find him true; And therefore, since his love is not for me, I'll help to make my rival's misery.

[*Aside.*

Spaniard, I never thought you false before:

[*To him.*

Can you at once two mistresses adore? Keep the poor soul no longer in suspense, Your change is such as does not need defence.

Cort. Riddles like these I cannot understand.

Alm. Why should you blush? she saw you kiss my hand.

Cyd. Fear not; I will, while your first love's denied, Favour your shame, and turn my eyes aside; My feeble hopes in her deserts are lost: I neither can such power nor beauty boast: I have no tie upon you to be true, But that, which loosened yours, my love to you.

Cort. Could you have heard my words!

Cyd. ——Alas, what needs To hear your words, when I beheld your deeds ?

Cort. What shall I say ? the fate of love is such, That still it sees too little or too much. That act of mine, which does your passion move, Was but a mark of my respect, not love.

Alm. Vex not yourself excuses to prepare: For one, you love not, is not worth your care.

Cort. Cruel Almeria, take that life you gave; Since you but worse destroy me, while you save.

Cyd. No, let me die, and I'll my claim resign; For while I live, methinks, you should be mine.

Cort. The bloodiest vengeance, which she could pursue, Would be a trifle to my loss of you.

Cyd. Your change was wise: for, had she been denied, A swift revenge had followed from her pride: You from my gentle nature had no fears, All my revenge is only in my tears.

Cort. Can you imagine I so mean could prove, To save my life by changing of my love?

Cyd. Since death is that which naturally we shun, You did no more than I, perhaps, had done.

Cort. Make me not doubt, fair soul, your constancy; You would have died for love, and so would I.

Alm. You may believe him; you have seen it proved.

Cort. Can I not gain belief how I have loved? What can thy ends, malicious beauty, be: Can he, who kill'd thy brother, live for thee?

[*A noise of clashing of swords.*

[Vasquez *within, Indians against him.*

Vasq. Yield, slaves, or die; our swords shall force our way.

[*Within.*

Ind. We cannot, though o'er-powered, our trust betray.

[*Within.*

Cort. 'Tis Vasquez' voice, he brings me liberty.

Vasq. In spite of fate I'll set my general free;

[*Within.*

Now victory for us, the town's our own.

Alm. All hopes of safety and of love are gone: As when some dreadful thunder-clap is nigh, The winged fire shoots swiftly through the sky, Strikes and consumes, ere scarce it does appear, And by the sudden ill prevents the fear: Such is my state in this amazing woe, It leaves no power to think, much less to do. ——But shall my rival live, shall she enjoy That love in peace, I laboured to destroy?

[Aside.

Cort. Her looks grow black as a tempestuous wind; Some raging thoughts are rolling in her mind.

Alm. Rival, I must your jealous thoughts remove, You shall, hereafter, be at rest for love.

Cyd. Now you are kind.

Alm. ——He whom you love is true: But he shall never be possest by you.

[Draws her dagger, and runs towards her.

Cort. Hold, hold, ah barbarous woman! fly, oh fly!

Cyd. Ah pity, pity, is no succour nigh!

Cort. Run, run behind me, there you may be sure, While I have life, I will your life secure.

[Cydaria gets behind him.

Alm. On him, or thee,—light vengeance anywhere

[She stabs and hurts him.

——What have I done? I see his blood appear!

Cyd. It streams, it streams from every vital part: Was there no way but this to find his heart?

Alm. Ah! cursed woman, what was my design! This weapon's point shall mix that blood with mine!

[Goes to stab herself, and being within his reach he snatches the dagger.

Cort. Now neither life nor death are in your power.

Alm. Then sullenly I'll wait my fatal hour.

Enter Vasquez and Pizarro, with drawn swords.

Vasq. He lives, he lives.

Cort. ——Unfetter me with speed; Vasquez, I see you troubled that I bleed: But 'tis not deep, our army I can head.

Vasq. You to a certain victory are led; Your men, all armed, stand silently within : I with your freedom did the work begin.

Piz. What friends we have, and how we came so strong, We'll softly tell you as we march along.

Cort. In this safe place let me secure your fear:

[To Cydaria.

No clashing swords, no noise can enter here. Amidst our arms as quiet you shall be, As Halcyons brooding on a winter sea.

Cyd. Leave me not here alone, and full of fright, Amidst the terrors of a dreadful night: You judge, alas, my courage by your own; I never durst in darkness be alone: I beg, I throw me humbly at your feet.——

Cort. You must not go where you may dangers meet The unruly sword will no distinction make; And beauty will not there give wounds, but take.

Alm. Then stay and take me with you; tho' to be A slave to wait upon your victory. My heart unmoved can noise and horror bear: Parting from you is all the death I fear.

Cort. Almeria, 'tis enough I leave you free: You neither must stay here, nor go with me.

Alm. Then take my life, that will my rest restore: Tis all I ask, for saving yours before.

Cort. That were a barbarous return of love.

Alm. Yet, leaving it, you more inhuman prove. In both extremes I some relief should find; Oh! either hate me more, or be more kind.

Cort. Life of my soul, do not my absence mourn: But cheer your heart in hopes of my return.

[*To* Cyd.

Your noble father's life shall be my care; And both your brothers I'm obliged to spare.

Cyd. Fate makes you deaf, while I in vain implore;— My heart forebodes, I ne'er shall see you more: I have but one request,—when I am dead, Let not my rival to your love succeed.

Cort. Fate will be kinder than your fears foretell; Farewell, my dear.

Cyd. ——A long and last farewell: —So eager to employ the cruel sword? Can you not one, not one last look afford!

Cort. I melt to womanish tears, and if I stay, I find my love, my courage will betray, Yon tower will keep you safe, but be so kind To your own life, that none may entrance find.

Cyd. Then lead me there.——

[*He leads her.*

For this one minute of your company, I go, methinks, with some content to die.

[*Exeunt* Cortez, Vasquez, Pizarro, *and* Cydaria

Alm. Farewell, O too much loved, since loved in vain! What dismal fortune does for me remain! Night and despair my fatal footsteps guide; That chance may give the death which he denied.

[*Exit.*

Cortez, Vasquez, Pizarro, *and Spaniards return again.*

Cort. All I hold dear I trust to your defence;

[*To Piz.*

Guard her, and on your life, remove not hence.

[*Exeunt* Cortez *and* Vasquez.

Piz. I'll venture that—— The gods are good; I'll leave her to their care, Steal from my post, and in the plunder share.

[*Exit.*

ACT V.

SCENE I.—*A chamber royal, an Indian hammock discovered in it.*

{{*Enter* Odmar *with soldiers,* Guyomar, *and* Alibech *bound.*}}

Odm. Fate is more just than you to my desert, And in this act you blame, heaven takes my part

Guy. Can there be gods, and no revenge provide?

Odm. The gods are ever of the conquering side: She's now my queen; the Spaniards have agreed, I to my father's empire shall succeed.

Alib. How much I crowns contemn, I let thee see, Choosing the younger, and refusing thee.

Guy. Were she ambitious, she 'd disdain to own The pageant pomp of such a servile throne; A throne, which thou by parricide dost gain, And by most base submission must retain.

Alib. I loved thee not before; but, Odmar, know, That now I hate thee, and despise thee too.

Odm. With too much violence you crimes pursue, Which if I acted, 'twas for love of you. This, if it teach not love, may teach you fear: I brought not sin so far, to stop it here. Death in a lover's mouth would sound but ill: But know, I either must enjoy, or kill.

Alib. Bestow, base man, thy idle threats elsewhere, My mother's daughter knows not how to fear. Since, Guyomar, I must not be thy bride, Death shall enjoy what is to thee denied.

Odm. Then take thy wish.——

Guy. Hold, Odmar, hold: My right in Alibech I will resign: Rather than see her die, I 'll see her thine.

Alib. In vain thou wouldst resign, for I will be, Even when thou leav'st me, constant still to thee: That shall not save my life : Wilt thou appear Fearful for her, who for herself wants fear?

Odm. Her love to him shows me a surer way: I by her love her virtue must betray.——

[*Aside.*

Since, Alibech, you are so true a wife,

[*To her.*

'Tis in your power to save your husband's life: The gods, by me, your love and virtue try; For both will suffer, if you let him die.

Alib. I never can believe you will proceed To such a black, and execrable deed.

Odm. I only threatened you; but could not prove So much a fool, to murder what I love: But in his death I some advantage see: Worse than it is I 'm sure it cannot be. If you consent, you with that gentle breath Preserve his life: If not, behold his death.

[*Holds his sword to his breast.*

Alib. What shall I do!

Guy. What, are your thoughts at strife About a ransom to preserve my life? Though to save yours I did my interest give, Think not, when you were his, I meant to live.

Alib. O let him be preserved by any way: But name not the foul price which I must pay.

[*To* Odm.

Odm. You would, and would not,—I'll no longer stay.

[*Offers again to kill him.*

Alib. I yield, I yield ; but yet, ere I am ill, An innocent desire I would fulfil: With Guyomar I one chaste kiss would leave, The first and last he ever can receive.

Odm. Have what you ask: That minute you agree To my desires, your husband shall be free.

[*They unbind her, she goes to her husband.*

Guy. No, Alibech, we never must embrace.

[*He turns from her.*

Your guilty kindness why do you misplace? 'Tis meant to him, he is your private choice; I was made yours but by the public voice. And now you leave me with a poor pretence, That your ill act is for my life's defence.

Alib. Since there remains no other means to try, Think I am false ; I cannot see you die.

Guy. To give for me both life and honour too, Is more, perhaps, than I could give for you. You have done much to cure my jealousy, But cannot perfect it unless both die! For since both cannot live, who stays behind Must be thought fearful, or, what's worse, unkind.

Alib. I never could propose that death you choose; But am, like you, too jealous to refuse.

[*Embracing him.*

Together dying, we together show That both did pay that faith, which both did owe.

Odm. It then remains I act my own design: Have you your wills, but I will first have mine. Assist me, soldiers——

[*They go to bind her: She cries out.*

Enter Vasquez, *and two Spaniards.*

Vasq. Hold, Odmar, hold! I come in happy time To hinder my misfortune, and your crime.

Odm. You ill return the kindness I have shown.

Vasq. Indian, I say, desist.

Odm. Spaniard, be gone.

Vasq. This lady I did for myself design: Dare you attempt her honour, who is mine ?

Odm. You're much mistaken; this is she, whom I Did with my father's loss, and country's buy: She, whom your promise did to me convey, When all things else were made your common prey.

Vasq. That promise made, excepted one for me; One whom I still reserved, and this is she.

Odm. This is not she; you cannot be so base.

Vasq. I love too deeply to mistake the face: The vanquished must receive the victor's laws.

Odm. If I am vanquished, I myself am cause.

Vasq. Then thank yourself for what you undergo.

Odm. Thus lawless might does justice overthrow.

Vasq. Traitors, like you, should never justice name.

Odm. You owe your triumphs to that traitor's shame. But to your general Ill my right refer.

Vasq. He never will protect a ravisher: His generous heart will soon decide our strife; He to your brother will restore his wife. It rests we two our claim in combat try, And that with this fair prize the victor fly.

Odm. Make haste, I cannot suffer to be long perplext; Conquest is my first wish, and death my next.

> [*They fight, the Spaniards and Indians fight.*

Alib. The gods the wicked by themselves o'er throw: All fight against us now, and for us too!

> [*Unbinds her husband.*

> [*The two Spaniards and three Indians kill each other,* Vasquez *kills* Odmar, Guyomar *runs to his brothers sword.*

Vasq. Now you are mine; my greatest foe is slain.

> [*To* Al.

Guy. A greater still to vanquish does remain.

Vasq. Another yet! The wounds, I make, but sow new enemies, Which from their blood, like earth-born brethren, rise.

Guy. Spaniard, take breath: Some respite I'll afford, My cause is more advantage than your sword.

Vasq. Thou art so brave could it with honour be, I 'd seek thy friendship more than victory.

Guy. Friendship with him, whose hand did Odmar kill! Base as he was, he was my brother still: And since his blood has washed away his guilt, Nature asks thine for that which thou hast spilt.

> [*They fight a little and breathe,* Alibech *takes up a sword and comes on.*

Alib. My weakness may help something in the strife.

Guy. Kill not my honour to preserve my life:

> [*Staying her.*

Rather than by thy aid I'll conquest gain, Without defence I poorly will be slain.

> [*She goes back, they fight again,* Vasquez *falls.*

Guy. Now, Spaniard, beg thy life, and thou shall live.

Vasq. 'Twere vain to ask thee what thou canst not give; My breath goes out, and I am now no more; Yet her, I loved, in death I will adore.

> [*Dies.*

Guy. Come, Alibech, let us from hence remove. This is a night of horror, not of love. From every part I hear a dreadful noise, The vanquished crying, and the victor's joys. I'll to my father's aid and country's fly, And succour both, or in their ruin die.

[*Exeunt.*

EPILOGUE

BY A MERCURY.

To all and singular in this full meeting, Ladies and gallants, Phoebus sends ye greeting. To all his sons, by whate'er title known, Whether of court, or coffee-house, or town; From his most mighty sons, whose confidence Is placed in lofty sound, and humble sense, Even to his little infants of the time, Who write new songs, and trust in tune and rhyme: Be't known, that Phoebus (being daily grieved To see good plays condemned, and bad received) Ordains, your judgment upon every cause, Henceforth be limited by wholesome laws. He first thinks fit no sonnetteer advance His censure, farther than the song or dance. Your wit burlesque may one step higher climb, And in his sphere may judge all doggrel rhyme: All proves, and moves, and loves, and honours too; All that appears high sense, and scarce is low. As for the coffee-wits, he says not much; Their proper business is to damn the Dutch: For the great dons of wit— Phoebus gives them full privilege alone, To damn all others, and cry up their own. Last, for the ladies, 'tis Apollo's will, They should have power to save, but not to kill: For love and he long since have thought it fit, Wit live by beauty, beauty reign by wit.

THE END

Printed in the USA
CPSIA information can be obtained
at www.ICGtesting.com
LVHW070900051223
765540LV00005B/132